THE NEARLY NIXED NOËL

A LORA WEAVER MYSTERY NOVELLA

KATY LEEN

ISBN: print: 978-0-9877543-8-7

Cover design: Team KL

Cover illustration by Adrienne Alexander

Cover background icons: The Noun Project, Tree # 1998998

For the girls & guys upstairs.
And my mom,
who filled every Christmas of my childhood
with oranges, tourtières, and love.

"*H*OW DID I get stuck carrying the head?"

Camille Caron paused near the end of the driveway, her boots slipping slightly on the snow beneath them before coming to a complete stop. "*Heille là*, you want the feet, Lora? You can have the feet."

Now she tells me. I inched forward, forcing her to start walking again, her back facing the road, her steps close together.

"Hurry up, will you," I said to her. "This guy is heavy."

We scurried another few yards, stopping in front of the open trunk of Camille's silver Jetta. "You put your end in first," she said to me.

I hoisted the head as high as I could, bumping it on the rim as I hefted it into the trunk. "Ouch. Sorry, buddy. Lucky for you, you couldn't feel that."

Camille slid the rest of the body in and slammed the trunk closed.

"His hat is sticking out," I told her, pointing to a slip of red fabric flapping in the wind.

She opened the trunk, reached in, tucked the hat tail to the side of his head, and closed the trunk again.

"*Venez, les filles,*" a voice called out.

I turned to see Camille's mother, Sylvie, in the doorway of her small stone home. She waved her arm towards the house, snow drifting off the overhang above the door and landing on her sweater that beamed fluorescent green under the morning sun. "*Venez,*" she said again. "*Finissez vos chocolats chauds.*"

Yes. That sounded like a good idea, going back in the warm house and finishing our cocoa. Way better than driving this guy ninety miles away from Montreal and stashing him in a barn.

Camille trudged up to the house and I followed, already debating whether to have a maple tart with my cocoa or a butter cookie. Or maybe one of each. Hefting around a body was hard work.

"You need a better coat, Lora," Sylvie said to me, taking my jacket as Camille and I shed our outdoor gear down to our jeans, sweaters, and socks.

"Maybe a good duck one," Sylvie added as she reached up to hang our coats in the hall closet.

"You mean down, *maman*, not duck," Camille corrected her.

Sylvie was close enough with the "duck" as far as I was concerned. Camille's mom, like the rest of her family, spoke English when I was around, and her English was way better than my French. Since I'd arrived in Montreal, I'd realized I was very slow picking up new languages. I was starting to believe I'd been shorted the language gene at birth. Or maybe I'd traded it for double scoops of the ice cream-loving gene—I was very fluent in ice cream.

"And Lora doesn't do down, remember?" Camille went on. "She's *végétarienne.*" As she spoke, she fluffed up her short blonde hair, prompting me to do the same to my ginger mane. Hat hair was not a good winter look on either of us.

Sylvie waved a dismissive hand in the air as we walked towards the kitchen off the side of the main hall. "Your mother, rest her soul, would want you to be warm, Lora," she said to me. "What about wool? I have a good wool coat I can give you, blue like your eyes. It would be good, no?"

I smiled at the generous offer. "Thanks, Madame Caron. But I'm fine, really."

We all sat at the large oak table, and Sylvie poured out cocoa for each of us from a teapot. Then she passed around a plate of homemade cookies and tarts, set down the plate, and fixed me with knowing motherly eyes, a warm brown like the hair resting on her shoulders. "Your little jacket may have been fine when you lived in New York, but not for Montreal," she said. "And where you are going it is more cold than this."

I glanced at Camille as I chose some Christmas goodies and set them around the rim of my saucer. I knew *Trois-Rivières*, the town where we were headed, was a bit north of the city, but could it possibly be much colder? As it was, the minute I stepped outside, my nose ran and I practically had icicles forming under my nostrils. Any colder and I'd be walking around like a zombie, my legs too frozen to bend. Good thing I packed the new winter vest I'd gotten from my boyfriend Adam as a pre-Christmas gift, and I could layer it on under my coat if Madame Caron was right about the drop in temperature.

Camille reached for a cookie from the serving plate. "She'll be fine, *maman*. We're only staying one night."

A door near the back of the kitchen opened, and in walked Camille's brother Laurent followed by her father Édouard. Both men were smiling and red cheeked, Laurent dressed in jeans and a black, long-sleeved t-shirt, Édouard wearing gray slacks and a red turtleneck. The latter with thinning hair and a clean shave in contrast to Laurent's thick, dark hair halfway to his shoulders and permanent scruff.

"Staying where for one night?" Laurent asked, his nearly black eyes glinting as he snatched a tart from my plate.

"*Vraiment*, Laurent," Camille said. "You're too old for listening at the door."

Laurent shrugged one shoulder and grinned. "I was not listening. I was helping papa fix a broken window in the sunroom. It's not my fault you're loud."

Loud had nothing to do with it. The man was a PI and an ex-cop. At close enough range, he could zero in on other people's conversations like the bionic woman. I learned this first hand over the eight months I'd worked as an assistant cum trainee at the PI agency he and Camille ran. And uncanny hearing was just one of Laurent's many skills I'd discovered so far—most of which left me grateful he was working the good side of the law.

Camille's eyes squinted at him, and I ventured into their conversation before it escalated into one of their sibling verbal matches. Or worse.

"We're going to your grandmother's house," I told Laurent, following my words with a sip of cocoa.

He took the chair next to mine and directed his next question at Camille. "*Chez grand-maman? Pourquoi?*"

"It was Lora's idea. We're helping wrap gifts for the Christmas toy drive."

I leaned forward and smiled. "*And*, we're bringing the guest of honor for the Christmas Eve party after the family church services."

Camille's dad went over to the sink and washed his hands, pulling a towel from a hook to dry them as he turned back to us. "Ah, that explains the empty coffin."

"*Oui*," Camille said. "And I refuse to put him back into it when it's all over. Keeping *Père Noël* in a coffin is creepy."

Creepy didn't begin to describe how I'd felt lifting Santa's body out of a coffin and tossing him into Camille's trunk. If I was a kid, I'd be worried about coal in my stocking this year for sure.

Sylvie got up and got two more mugs for the late arrivals. "It's not creepy, it saves space. It's you kids who wanted to keep all the Halloween decorations. Me, I'd be happy with only the Christmas ones."

Laurent took the cup his mother offered him and poured cocoa into it. "Your Anglophone is not going to help, Lora?"

By my Anglophone, Laurent meant Adam, the boyfriend I moved from New York to Montreal with two years earlier. I shook my head. "He can't. He's in California on business."

Laurent's left eyebrow edged up and he slipped a tart from my plate. "A business trip three days before Christmas?"

"Uh huh," I said, grabbing a sprinkle-coated shortbread cookie in the shape of a star and shoving it in my mouth to avoid saying more. Adam and I had argued about that very thing, but he was supposed to be home before Christmas Eve and the trip couldn't be helped. Some last-minute snafu with a computer game he'd designed that was due to be presented to the investors by New Year's. The timing was poor to say the least, and I would have had to back out of helping with the toy drive, too, if our neighbor hadn't agreed to pet sit our cat Ping and dog Pong for the night.

"*Pauvre*, Lora," Laurent said as he leaned towards me and took a cookie off my plate, his warm, maple breath skimming my cheek. "Left all alone to prepare for the holiday. I'd be happy to help. Maybe trim your tree? String your lights?"

This was not a bona fide offer. This was Laurent toying with me. He does that. I grabbed my cookie back from him. "I'm fine," I told him, biting into my cookie. "No need for any help at all, thank you."

He smiled and reached to take the last cookie from my plate, but Camille swatted his hand away.

"Enough," she said and stood up. "*Allez*, Lora. Let's go. We're supposed to be at *grand-maman's* for lunch, and it's already ten o'clock. It's a long drive and if it snows again, it will be even longer."

Laurent got up and stretched. "Maybe I will go also. I would like to see *grand-maman*."

"There's no room for you, big brother," Camille said, shooting him a look. "You'll have to wait until Christmas dinner to see her. The back seat is filled with toys for the kids."

Laurent smiled and shook his head at Camille. "*Ah oui*? Too bad."

After making pit stops by the washroom, saying our goodbyes, and stowing a few tins of Sylvie's tarts in the Jetta's trunk, Camille and I drove off with her family waving to us from the doorway. As I watched them get smaller in my side-view mirror, my eyes picked up a flash of red billowing out from the trunk. More of Santa's suit escaping again, no doubt.

2

TWO HOURS LATER, another flash of red hit my eyes. Only this time it was a strobe flaring from the top of a cop car.

Camille's hands tightened on the steering wheel, and she let out an impressive stream of Franglais expletives as she pulled the Jetta to the shoulder of the road. She buzzed the window down as the cop—dressed in dark clothes with dark glasses and an even darker attitude—swaggered over to the car.

He said something to Camille in French, his tone low and grave, his words strewn together.

"Piss off," Camille said back to him.

Instantly, my body sank down in my seat, my instincts one step ahead of the rest of me in spotting trouble coming. I loved that Camille was a woman never afraid to speak her mind, but sometimes it would be nice if her mind came with a remote for me with a rewind and edit switch.

The cop slid his sunglasses down to the bridge of his nose with the tip of his gloved finger. He dipped back and scanned the back seat then leaned forward, his head partially entering the open window. He looked past Camille at me then back at her. More French words spewed from his mouth, and he pulled his head back outside.

Camille rolled her eyes and reached down beside her.

I heard the trunk release click as Camille started to get out and follow the cop to the rear of the car. Before I could reconsider, I jumped out and joined them.

The cop had his sunglasses off by the time I took my place staring down at Santa in the trunk. Santa's head was bent where we'd had to wedge him in to make him fit, making him look as though his neck was devoid of bones. Or broken. And he had tins of tarts on his chest. Two tins decorated in Rudolphs and one in Frosty the Snowmans.

Camille and the cop exchanged a look and a few more words I couldn't quite make out—except for my name caught in the middle there somewhere.

The cop turned to me, and his eyes skimmed up to my hat and back to my face. He reached over and cupped the three tiny bells that had come loose from my purple pom-poms and sat drooping towards my right ear. "Careful, Lora. You're about to lose your jinglers."

Camille's arm swung out and whacked the cop in the belly. "*Laisse-la*," she said.

Even through all his layers, Camille's whack must have connected because the cop's face reddened some and his eyes showed he had been caught off guard. Most men were when it came to Camille. She was a knockout in more ways than one. But this time, I was thinking maybe she'd gone too far. Hitting a cop was serious business.

"I could haul you in for that," he said, slipping his sunglasses back on. He pulled a pad from his pocket. "But maybe I'll just write you up for your burned out brake light and transporting a body."

We all looked down at Santa again, our heads tilting slightly to the left.

I reached into the trunk and tried to straighten Santa's neck. "He's not a body. He's a doll," I said, turning to fix the cop with my best get-out-of-jail-free smile. "We can't be in trouble for transporting a doll, can we?"

The cop's mouth slowly pulled into a smile that didn't break when Camille stepped in front of him and slammed the trunk closed. "We're not in trouble for anything," she said. "This is my sick cousin's idea of a joke."

Cousin? Right. I should have guessed. Camille's brother Laurent used to be a cop. And her ex, Luc, was a cop. Why not her cousin? Probably she had lots of cop cousins given that most of her Roman Catholic family took the "fruitful and multiply" thing seriously.

"Good to finally meet you, Lora," the cop said. He extended his gloved hand to shake mine. "François."

Camille started back for the front of the Jetta. "Your name will be nothing when *grand-maman* finds out you made us late for lunch."

François shook his head and trailed me to the passenger side door, reaching around me to open it. "You won't let Camille tell her, will you Lora? Laurent said *you're* nice. As sweet on the inside as you are to look at on the outside."

I stopped, my body half in the car, and turned back to François. "Laurent said that?"

Camille sighed so loud I could hear it through my hat. She got in the Jetta and fired up the engine, revving it a few times, the car slipping forward slightly as I scrambled to get into my seat before she took off and left half of me on the sidewalk.

François muttered an answer to my question that got muffled by my hat before I could catch it. Then he closed my door and stepped away as we pulled out.

I looked back at him as the Jetta roared up the street, happy to see he'd stepped away fast enough to keep all his body parts intact.

"Don't pay any attention to François, Lora." Camille said. "He fell out of a tree when he was a kid and was unconscious for three hours. He hasn't been the same since. We all just humor him now."

I glanced at her as she drove, her eyes trained on the snowy road. "And you let him be a cop and carry a gun?"

"*Ben oui*. Why not?"

"Because you just implied he's loopy."

"*Non, non*, I said he's not the same. He was quiet and serious before the accident. Now he thinks he's a comedian and pushes his big nose into everyone's business."

The big nose bit was a crack. François had a perfect nose. And the same gleam in his eye Camille got when she discovered a new *chocolatier*. His chestnut brown hair was lighter than most Carons and he had dimples, but there was no mistaking the family resemblance in his eyes.

"And he's a show-off," Camille went on. "The big jerk had no reason to pull me over. He did that for you."

"For me? He doesn't even know me. And I think you're forgetting the broken brake light. Cops pull people over for stuff like that all the time."

"Pfft. One broken brake light. That's nothing. The other one works fine."

I glanced at her. "Your cousin must really get to you. You know brake lights aren't like kidneys. You can't get along with just one."

She blew out air. "*Peut-être*. But I *could* get along with one less cousin."

· · ·

10

FOR A LITTLE OLD LADY, Camille's grandmother had strong fingers that pinched my cheeks so hard I could barely feel the scratch of her chapped lips as she followed up her pinches with kisses. She wore a green, flowery housedress in a thick woven cotton below an apron imprinted with the three wise men carrying their gifts for the baby Jesus. And her huge kitchen smelled like cloves.

A timer buzzed, and *grand-maman*, as she insisted I call her, dashed over to her double-wide oven, pulled out four pies, and set them on racks resting on the counter. More pies lined the counters nearby. Enough pies to fill a small-town bakery. The room felt like one, too—warm and filled with walnut cabinets topped with marble counters. Open shelving lined the upper walls, the shelves filled with canisters and dishware. A large island stood dead center, and a long table with equally long benches filled an outcrop framed with windows with a view to the backyard. Walls were papered in a faded yellow flower pattern. And the floors were tiled in ceramic, uneven with age.

I sniffed the air, trying to place the scent of the pies. Not apple, not cherry, not blueberry. And no cinnamon wafting off them. I moved in for a closer peek. There was a miniature Christmas tree cut-out in the center of each pie revealing the filling. It was brown and savory smelling.

Camille came up beside me and leaned in for a strong whiff. "*Tourtière*," she said to me. "Meat pies. They're Caron tradition every Christmas and *grand-maman* makes them best." She stepped over to plant a kiss on her grandmother's cheek.

"Come," *grand-maman* said, brushing off the compliment as easily as she slipped off her apron and draped it over the back of a chair at the head of the table. She walked towards a door and out of the room. "There is much to do."

Camille and I followed her out. First, through a dining room that had a brick fireplace with built-in buffets on either side, a big table surrounded by high-back chairs, and bay windows over-looking the backyard. Then we moved on to a room with more bay windows, this time facing front. This room had another fire-place, a stone one, and a plump sofa, a compact piano, and enough rocking chairs to challenge Goldilocks' selection skills. The fire-place was flanked by a husky on one side and a German shepherd on the other, each curled up on a cushy dog bed. And according to Camille, each ancient and arthritic.

The husky, Princess, raised her head, blinked at us, and went back to sleep. Simon, the shepherd, did the same but added a hoarse bark before lowering his head.

Part of me was surprised the dogs weren't wearing reindeer antlers since so far *grand-maman's* house had me thinking it doubled as a Christmas shop. Everywhere I looked, there were garlands, festive figurines, candles, tiny decorated pine trees. None of it outdone by the elaborate nativity scenes that topped each fireplace mantel. What little else I'd seen of the rest of the house was equally decked out, complete with mistletoe hanging in every doorway. All that was missing were the Christmas carols. And maybe elves.

Of course, that's where we came in.

Grand-maman pushed open large pine pocket doors at the end of the living room, revealing what looked like a more modest space with worn plaid loveseats and a TV. Probably a den when the seating wasn't covered in shopping bags filled to overflowing with kids' paraphernalia.

"Each toy will need to be wrapped and labelled," *Grand-maman* said, moving into the room and getting down to business. She pointed to a pile of papers on the coffee table. "The list of names for all the kids is there. *Avec leurs âges*, eh, and for some, wish lists."

I picked up the papers and scanned them. The list was done

spreadsheet style over several pages and included lots of details, some written in English, some in French. Details someone who didn't know the kids personally would never include. But *grand-maman* had been a schoolteacher before she retired years before, and she was running the toy drive through her church where she helped out year-round with the little parishioners. Like the rest of the huge Caron clan, *grand-maman* was Catholic. And although most of the younger generation of the family wasn't so active in the church, all the Carons still respected their elders who were. Like *grand-maman*.

I was more spiritual than religious, but I'd been brought up with Christmas and was happy she let me play a role in helping local kids have a good holiday. Especially as an ex-social worker who still remained one at heart even if I didn't get paid for it anymore. Well, unless you counted my job at Camille and Laurent's PI agency, C&C. Which I definitely did count. Privately. Publicly, I was a PI in training. But privately, I thought a lot of PI work was social work in disguise. At least the way I did it.

Camille took one look at the mounds of toy-filled bags and stroked her stomach. "What about lunch, *grand-maman*? *Je meurs de faim.*"

Grand-maman reached out and squeezed Camille's shoulder, working her squeezes down to Camille's elbow. "*Bien sûr*. Of course, you're hungry. You're skin and bones." She released Camille and pointed at me. "And you, too." Then she narrowed her eyes at Camille. "But lunch finished already. You're late."

"That's not my fault," Camille told her. "François played big cop for Lora. You know what he's like."

Grand-maman's face turned stern. "*Ça suffit, là!* Camille. François is a good boy. You need to forget the past and give him a chance." She turned and walked back into the living room. "Now you girls start work. I'll get you something to eat when I am done with the pies."

I glanced at Camille, expecting her to protest and plead for the lunch before we started in on the toys. But she said nothing. Until *grand-maman* was out of earshot. Then Camille muttered something to herself in French about decorating François' neck with a garland. Although I may have misunderstood the decorating bit.

3

AMILLE AND I had long since used up the calories from the soup and baguette *grand-maman* served us for a late lunch, and we had everything wrapped when *grand-maman* announced that there were more toys in the barn. Lots more. And she wanted us to take this load to the church basement and hide it all, then get started on the next batch.

I had two problems with that plan: One, Camille had made for a sulky elf partner since she was still brooding about her cousin and refusing to explain *grand-maman*'s crack about the past; and two, no way would we be able to transport all the gifts in Camille's Jetta. Not without crushing the wrapping and bows. And not without making several trips. Not to mention the small issue of Santa taking up all the room in the trunk.

"Not to worry," Camille said to me after a brief debate of how we could solve problem number two. "There's a pickup truck in the barn. We can use that."

She snatched a set of keys near the back door, and we geared up for the great outdoors again and trudged over to the barn.

Grand-maman's house was on the outskirts of *Trois-Rivières*, and the property had come with several outbuildings and an old barn that probably nobody used for at least fifty years. At least that was my best guess judging by the decaying rafters, lack of heat, layers of dust, and what I was pretty sure was a family of bats nesting in the hayloft.

"Oh my," I said, spying a palette piled high and wide with various toys and kid stuff. My heart filled with glee at the thought of all the kids who would be the happy recipients of that bounty, and my head filled with panic at the realization that we would never get everything wrapped in time. "You know, it would save us time if we just stored the stuff that's ready here while we do each batch. Then we could take it all over at once."

"*Oui, oui,*" Camille agreed. She went to open the double barn doors, climbed into the pickup truck, and started the engine. "*Parfait.* It still works."

The edge of surprise in her voice didn't surprise me; the truck looked like it hadn't been used in nearly as long as the barn.

She stopped the truck, got out, and pulled the tarp from the back, careful to fold it inward to contain its collection of dust. We loaded up some toys and drove to the house to unload the haul and exchange it for the wrapped batch. It took several more trips back and forth and even more hours, with barely a dinner break, until we were all done. Just in time for bed.

"**WHAT DO YOU** mean we have to take it over now?" I asked Camille. "It's nearly midnight."

She stood and surveyed the packages we'd assembled near the wall that housed the TV in the den. "*Exactement.* It's perfect. All the kids are at home in bed. No one will see us."

Good point. Unfortunately. I so didn't feel like lugging packages off to church in the middle of the night. I ambled into the living room and helped myself to one of the chocolate-covered mint wafers *grand-maman* had left in an arrangement on an end table by the couch. My eyes trailed to the couch with its plump cushions and floral print throw, wondering if Camille would notice if I slipped under the blanket and hid.

"Don't even think about it," she said, coming up behind me and grabbing a wafer off the pedestal dish.

"Just a short nap?"

"*Non.*" She grabbed some chocolates and shoved them at me. "These are better than a nap."

Another good point. I made a sandwich out of the wafers and took a bite as we headed to the kitchen to fetch our coats.

When we got to the barn, Camille flicked a switch and multiple sconce-style lanterns on the side walls fizzled on, dotting the space in dim light. Perfect for a romantic *rendez-vous*. Not so perfect for spotting things that fly by in the night.

I gave the hayloft a quick look before focussing on the gifts. "We can't just pile all this stuff in the pickup. Everything will get crushed and it will never fit." Plus, we'd still need to make several trips. We could only pile things so high in the pickup bed or some could drop out on the way over to the church. I so did not want to be ferrying gifts all night. I was no Mrs. Claus.

"There's no other choice," Camille said. "I'll go get the last batch and you start sorting these by size so we can load fast when I get back." She climbed into the pickup and was off.

I checked the hayloft for movement again then got to work. I was in the middle of wrangling a giant stuffed panda when the lights near the gift pile went out. Fabulous. Now I had to work in the cold *and* the dark.

A fluttering sound caught my attention and I crouched, sure it was a bat. I held my breath and listened again. Nothing, so I scurried over to a light fixture and reached up to try tightening the bulb, but I couldn't reach it. A line of barrels were to my right and I thought one might make a promising stool, so I dragged the last one over and scrambled on top. Bingo. It brought me up high enough to slip my hand into the glass lantern and twist the bulb, which to my relief came on after only two turns, not burnt out just loose.

I shimmied the barrel over to the other darkened lantern and did the same. As I slid down from the barrel and scooted it back to join its brethren, I had an idea. I lifted the lid and peered inside. Clean and dry. Faint, pleasant smell. I checked a few of the others and found them in the same condition. Perfect.

I started gathering the kids' packages and distributing them among the barrels, packing them so there was plenty of air and nothing got crushed. Some of the stuffed animals were large and took up nearly a whole barrel, but they made ideal cushioning for smaller, more fragile gifts.

By the time I pushed the lid closed on my fifth barrel, the pickup was backing into the barn.

Camille hopped out of the truck and frowned at the leftover gifts. "*Mais voyons*. What happened to all the presents?"

I grinned. Not only did the barrels make excellent transportation containers, but clearly they'd make excellent hiding places once we got our packages to the church. Double score. That would save time and we could be back and tucked up in bed all the sooner.

"Right here," I told her, pointing to the barrels.

"You put them in the old maple syrup tubs?"

Maple syrup tubs? So that was the scent I'd picked up on.

She walked over and knocked at one. "They're heavy. How will we get them up into the pickup?"

Hmm. Hadn't thought of that. 'They're not that bad," I told her.

"Most of the gifts are pretty light and don't add much weight. If you back up the truck real close, the two of us should be able to manage."

She raised her eyebrows at me and went on to tip the packed barrels a bit, testing their weight, letting out a sigh when she was done.

"We could call your cousin to help?" I suggested. It was late and all, but he was a cop. Probably he got lots of emergency calls at night. And this was kind of an emergency.

Camille spun around and faced me. "*Non. Absolument pas.*" She rubbed her gloved hands together. "We'll be fine."

She set to packing another barrel, and between the two of us we had eight packed and ready to go soon after. Hefting them into the pickup took us longer. Camille worked the heavier end from the floor, and I hoisted them from inside the flatbed and half pushed and half rocked them into place.

Then Camille shut off the lights and closed up the barn doors, and we got into the pickup.

We were halfway down the long path to the road when I realized we'd left our guest of honor behind.

TEN MINUTES LATER, Santa was nestled in his own barrel and loaded onto the truck, and we were chugging along en route to church when the pickup began to sputter. Camille maneuvered it to the side of the road and cut the engine.

Whatever meagre heat we had in the cab ebbed away instantly thanks to a crack in the back window.

"Maybe the truck just needs a little rest?" I said hopefully, pulling my hat down over my ears as far as it would go and suppressing a yawn that was working its way into a groan. "Maybe it's tired because it hasn't been used in a while?"

"*Non, non,*" Camille said. "*Probablement* it needs gas."

I eyed her. "Probably?"

"*C'est possible* the gas tank was low. The red line was on E when we left *grand-maman's.*"

"Then why didn't you get gas at the station we passed a couple miles back?"

Camille waved her arm in the air. "Everybody knows there's plenty of gas left when the line hits E. We should have made our delivery and gone home fine. Something must be wrong with the truck."

I sighed. Only Camille could use that logic and say it like she believed it.

She reached into the small area behind the front seat and swore. Her lack of purse likely hitting her about now. Ergo her lack of cell phone. Ditto for me. We'd left our purses at *grand-maman's* when we'd gone out to organize the gifts, and I for one never thought about retrieving mine when we'd loaded up the truck and headed off for Galilee. Or at least the nearest thing to Galilee a person could find in *Trois-Rivières*, Québec.

"What do we do now?" I asked her, peering through the haze starting to cover my window, trying to make out our surroundings. "Looks like there's a bar on the corner up ahead. Maybe it's still open and we could use their phone."

"There's no one close enough to call," Camille said. "I don't want to wake *grand-maman.* She does too much at the holidays and needs her rest. And her sister and her husband are in Florida visiting their kids."

I fingered the door handle. "There's your cousin?"

"I'm not calling François. He'd tell the story for the rest of his life." She opened her door and started to get out of the truck. "*Allez.* We'll find someone in the bar to help."

Getting help from bar goers still wolfing back drinks in the wee hours of the morning did not appeal to me. But neither did sitting in the pickup with my toes freezing off. It's hard to walk without toes.

Ten minutes and a little eye batting later, we left the bar with Hugo, the assistant bartender. His speech didn't slur, his feet moved in a straight line, and he was able to zip up his parka in one swift move. Plus, he was an old Sunday school student of *grand-maman's* and had promised to fetch us some gas at the twenty-four hour station a few blocks away.

Camille and I trundled back to the truck to wait for our knight in Gore Tex armor. Only there was no truck at the end of our trundle. Just a long, empty space between a blue mini-van and a rusted sedan. I remembered the mini van being there when we left but not the sedan.

It was unlikely we were towed for violating parking laws or snow clearing rules if the other two cars weren't, but my eyes traveled up to the parking sign anyway just to be sure. My eyes met Camille's after she did the same then shook her head.

"*Incroyable,*" she said.

I agreed. It was incredible. Who would want a beat up old pickup? And how did whoever did take off so fast in a truck that had no gas?

We were still staring at the vacant spot when Hugo showed up, a plastic tub in hand, a faint smell of gasoline oozing from his general direction.

While Hugo and Camille slipped into a conversation in French, presumably about the missing truck, I wandered over to check out the sedan. No license plate in the front. No biggie since Québec plates went in the back, the front left bare or sporting personalized monikers or the like. But there was no back plate on the sedan, either. Just more rust and a dent in the bumper. I shifted to the car doors and peered inside. With the frosted windows, it was tough to see much, but from what I could make out it was in worse shape than the exterior. And stripped clean.

Camille stepped over to give the sedan a once-over, too, Hugo trailing after her. When she was done, she kicked the front tire and the hubcap fell off.

"What are we going to do?" I said, panic making its way to my voice. "All the toys are gone and it's only two days until Christmas."

"Not to worry." Camille reached her arm across the back of my shoulders and squeezed lightly. "We'll find them."

She nodded over at Hugo who set down the plastic tub and pulled a phone from his pocket.

4

"*V*OYONS, FRANÇOIS," CAMILLE said. "How hard can it be to find? *Grand-maman's* truck is beyond old. It should be easy to spot." She sat back on the chair in *grand-maman's* kitchen and jabbed a sausage with her fork, cutting a piece and eating it.

I pushed scrambled eggs around on my plate and added in my two cents. "And the truck had no gas. How far could the thief get without gas? And what would he want with an old, gasless pickup anyway? It wasn't some kind of classic was it?"

"Ladies," François said, his head hunched over his plate, both hands working his breakfast, talking between swallows. "Probably the thief did not care about the truck. Probably he wanted the cargo."

Cargo? A bunch of kids' toys? I felt heat rise up my neck. "Seriously? How low can a person get to steal a bunch of toys. At Christmastime no less."

François sat upright and reached for another warm biscuit

from the basket *grand-maman* had filled. He shook his head. "Not toys, Lora. Maple syrup."

Hmm. I was starting to see what Camille meant about her cousin. Maybe the guy was a bit loopy. "Excuse me?"

"Maple syrup. The pickup was filled with maple syrup barrels, no?"

I nodded.

He sat back and swiped a napkin across his mouth, his eyes darting from me to Camille. He dropped his napkin and smiled, one hand rubbing his tummy, the other stretched out to rest on the empty bench space to his side.

His body language said the conclusion was obvious. Which it wasn't. At least to me. But I could see light dawning in Camille's eyes.

"*Ben oui, c'est sûr,*" she said, sliding her empty plate forward and resting her forearms on the table. "*Le sirop d'érable.*" She nodded her chin at me. "How many tubs did we fill, Lora?"

I gave it some thought. "Eight, I think. No, nine with Santa."

Her eyes lowered and moved in their sockets like she was in deep REM sleep. "That's at least 50 gallons each. At about 35 dollars a gallon, that's $1750 dollars each. That makes it—"

"Worth almost sixteen thousand dollars," François finished for her.

She raised her eyes and glared at him. When he smiled back, she glared harder until his smile faded.

"Are you saying that if the tubs had been filled with maple syrup that the whole lot would have been worth sixteen thousand dollars?" I asked.

Camille turned to me, her eyes returning to normal. "*Oui, c'est ça.*"

Okay, if that was true, that meant the thief was likely only greedy and not a complete dolt depriving kids of Christmas. Still, stealing maple syrup. What were the chances?

"Seems unlikely. Who would know a few barrels would be worth so much?" I said.

François stood and adjusted his uniform, his gun belted to him bulking up his right hip. "This is Québec. Everybody knows," he said. "Québec makes about 75 percent of the world's maple syrup. It brings in hundreds of millions of dollars a year."

Wow. Seventy-five percent. No country in the world could claim that about oil. This had to be a joke. Maple syrup could not be that big a deal. "Right. Next you're going to tell me there's some big hush hush bunker somewhere where the government secretly stockpiles the stuff, too. You know, so the world doesn't run out."

Camille and François exchanged a look. One of their few devoid of animosity.

"But of course," Camille said. "Millions of dollars worth are in reserves. The world counts on us for their supplies. We have to make sure we can deliver."

François nodded. "Over twenty million dollars of it was stolen from the reserves a while ago. It was a big problem. A priority case for the police."

I looked from one to the other of them, taking in their sombre expressions, and realized they weren't putting me on. They were serious. Which meant the idea of our thief taking the pickup thinking it was full of maple syrup wasn't sounding so funny. Or unlikely.

Then I had another realization that was even more disturbing. Since it was my brilliant idea to put the toys in the maple syrup barrels, it also made the theft my fault.

I felt my own expression turning sombre when an image went through my head of unhappy kids' faces with nothing to open Christmas morning.

I pushed back from the table and stood, too, leaving most of my breakfast uneaten. I had no appetite and no time to waste. I couldn't live with myself if the flash of disappointed kids became reality. I just had to get the toys back. And fast.

5

*I*T WAS LATE afternoon, and the toys were still missing. The sedan with no license plates was no help —it turned out to be stolen with no clues as to who left it behind. And Camille and I had retraced our steps, canvassed the neighborhood where *grand-maman's* truck was taken, and done a street-by-street drive-by checking driveways and yards for signs of the pickup or the barrels. Nothing. All we netted for our efforts was a lackey—Hugo, our knight in Gore Tex armor who attached himself to Camille like static cling on silk when we dropped by the bar in search of possible witnesses.

"Wait," Hugo said in his heavy French accent when once again Camille and I tried to leave. "I remember another thing about the two men. The little one had a limp."

The two men Hugo referred to were patrons of the bar the night before. Patrons who left moments after we came in. And patrons he assured us were not regulars.

Camille turned her barstool forward and eyed Hugo. This was the third time we'd been about to leave when Hugo *remembered* something new. This time she waited a beat before asking, "Anything else?"

Hugo's face went pensive then brightened. "They paid with money."

"Cash you mean, not bank card?" Camille clarified.

He nodded with enthusiasm. "Yes, cash only."

A man at the end of the bar held up an empty beer mug and gestured for Hugo. When the man got no response, he put two fingers in his mouth and blew out a whistle loud enough to make glassware hanging overhead jangle and to bring a middle-aged soft, sweaty man with a Brillo pad of salt-and-pepper hair come running out from the back.

The man stopped feet from the bar, hiked up his slack pants, and darted his eyes around the room before zeroing in on Hugo, still hunkered down, his arms leaning on the bar top, his gaze on Camille.

Stomping a few feet closer, the older man barked something at Hugo in French, and Hugo flushed red and bolted to attend the customer with the shrill whistle and empty mug.

Camille grabbed her bag from the bar top and slid off her stool. "*Allez*. We're done here."

I moved to follow her, feeling Hugo's eyes trailing us as we wound our way through the increasing crowd. Something tugged at my coat and Camille got a few steps ahead of me. I looked down to see what snagged me and saw fingers gripping my coat hem. Slender fingers with pristine purple nail polish sprinkled with tiny silver stars. The fingers belonged to a young woman sitting with a group of other young women at a round table, the bunch of them clustered in tight, their chairs squished together at off angles, their glasses filled with frothy white liquid.

"I saw them," the woman said to me when our eyes connected.

"Who?" I asked, thinking she had mistaken me for someone.

Easy to do in a crowded, dimly lit bar. Especially for someone who, judging by the glaze filming her eyes and the slight weave of her head as she spoke, had already had one eggnog too many.

"The men Hugo was telling you about," she said, more purr than slur to her voice, a faint indiscernible accent seeping through. "They tried to pick Amy and me up." Her eyes flitted to a girl with a shot of pink running down either side of her long, dark blonde hair. "They said they were from Chicoutimi. Here to visit their father for Christmas."

I nodded my understanding and leaned in to talk more. "They give you names? Or say who their dad was?"

"Only first names. Pierre and Gaétan."

The woman with pink in her hair cut into our interchange, her accent French, her voice scratchy. "They told me their dad owned Beaulieu's."

"What's that?"

"Mechanics place," purple nail polish girl said. "So what'd the guys do?"

I shrugged. "Not sure. Someone stole our pickup truck last night. Hugo thought it might be those guys."

"Wouldn't surprise me," Pink said. "Anything they got, they probably had to steal. They weren't too bright. Dropouts I'm sure."

My social worker side bristled at those last remarks. Judgmental assumptions had no place in social work. But the budding PI side of me thanked the women for their help and got descriptions of Pierre and Gaétan before I left to find Camille waiting for me at the door.

NON, NON. I am not taking my car to a mechanic to have the tail-light fixed," Camille said, driving the Jetta along the streets of *Trois-Rivières*.

"But this is the only lead we've got, and it's the perfect excuse to check out the Beaulieu garage."

Camille went quiet and pulled a foil-wrapped mint chocolate from her pocket when we stopped for a red light. She unwrapped the chocolate and popped it in her mouth.

I waited for the chocolate to seep into her system before trying again. We'd already gone by the Beaulieu house and found nothing. Nobody home and no signs on the property of the Beaulieu brothers, *grand-maman's* pickup, or the toys. The Beaulieu garage was the next logical step. Camille knew that as well as I did.

Plus, bonus, we'd get the light fixed. Which so far Camille had shown no signs of doing herself. I knew ordinarily she would have by now if it hadn't been her cousin who pointed out it was broken in the first place. Now she was leaving it to make a point. What kind of point I wasn't sure. Knowing Camille it fell into "you're not the boss of me" territory.

"*C'est ridicule,*" Camille said. "People will think I can't fix the light myself."

I turned to the side window so Camille wouldn't see me roll my eyes. Technically, *Trois-Rivières* was a city, but it was smaller than many suburbs and definitely had more of a town feel—I'd give Camille that. But it wasn't *that* small and no one was going to notice or care whether Camille fixed her own car or not.

"I saw that," she said, rejoining traffic when the light switched to green.

"Well, seriously, what does it matter what people think?"

She accelerated the Jetta, and I tightened my seat belt and watched her hands twist at the steering wheel as she toggled between lanes.

Stores decked out for Christmas with giant candy canes and wreaths whizzed by outside. Inside, the temperature dipped low enough to make Frosty the Snowman dance about with glee.

"We can question Beaulieu without an excuse," Camille finally said as she slowed the car to turn into a long lane leading to a ramshackle one-storey building. Small colored lights shaped out to spell *Joyeux Noël* flickered above a glass front at one end.

"Sure," I agreed. "But it would be less conspicuous if we were customers."

Camille got out, waited for me, then zapped the Jetta locked with her remote. We approached the glass front, almost half the *Joyeux Noël* lights above the door burned out and the fluorescents lights inside in an equal state. Two men sat in scuffed plastic and metal chairs lining the back wall. The counter, white once upon a time now smudged to beige, was untended. A small silver bell the only visible attempt at a receptionist.

The men in chairs nodded greetings to us as we went up to the counter. One man had arms crossed over his closed jacket, the other fiddled with his cell phone.

Camille punched the little silver bell and tapped her foot on the vinyl-tiled floor.

A petite older woman slipped through a door behind the counter and bustled over. Her mishmash hair had that yellow twinge that comes from a home dye job, and her pants were poly-ester. Her sweater a loose-knit blue acrylic that drooped.

"*Oui?*" she said.

Camille asked her if we could see Monsieur Beaulieu and was told he was busy on a car at the moment. More French words I didn't understand so well were exchanged, ending in the woman shaking her head and pursing her lips.

"*Excuse-moi, Madame,*" I said in my pitiful French. "*Parlez-vous anglais?*"

The woman tipped her head back & forth slightly, and I took that as a yes.

"We don't mean to bother Monsieur Beaulieu, but my friend

here really needs his help. She has a broken tail-light and the police told her to have it fixed right away or she'd get a ticket."

The woman slid her eyes to Camille and back to me.

I could feel Camille's stance stiffening beside me, but I plunged on before she reached out to wring my neck. "I'm sure for a man like Monsieur Beaulieu, the repair would be fast. And my friend really can't afford a ticket. You know, because of Christmas."

The woman's lips softened as she pinched them in her teeth at the corner.

I smiled at her. "Please. It will just take a few minutes. We still have errands to run for my friend's grandmother and we know that policeman is just waiting for us."

I could feel Camille's eyes narrowing to a squint and boring my way, but I refused to meet her glare. The darkening of her eyes was like an eclipse of the sun. Probably I'd risk blindness if I looked at her directly.

The woman held up a finger and said, *"Une minute."* Then she disappeared behind the door, coming out again a few minutes later with a harried, fiftysomething man in dirty coveralls and a head of thick black hair, gray at the temples. Underneath his bushy eyebrows, his blue eyes were piercing and lined into permanent slits.

"Oui?" he said, his accent thick with a lyrical twang.

I tried to explain our predicament, but the mechanic's face stayed blank. So I nudged Camille who let out a long sigh then explained in French about the broken light, and we all traipsed outside to look at it.

After a brief conversation with Monsieur Beaulieu and a few grumblings thrown my way, Camille drove her Jetta into the garage bay at the far end. From the looks of it, the bay didn't extend quite as far back as the office side of the building which meant searching it for *grand-maman's* pickup shouldn't be too hard. There weren't a lot of places to hide a truck.

"This is getting us nothing," Camille said to me as I moved to get out of the car. "He'll be done in two minutes and then what?"

"I don't know," I said. "Do what you always do, flirt or something. And I'll look around."

She let out another slow, long breath, and I suspected she was getting ready for a rant.

I shot her a bright smile, hoping to curtail her. After all, the best defense is always a happy offense, right?

She looked at me, shook her head, popped another one of her mint chocolates, and got out of the car.

6

CAMILLE CHUCKED OFF her boots and threw her purse onto *grand-maman's* kitchen table. "Did we get any information from Monsieur Beaulieu? *Non*. Did we see Gaétan or Pierre? *Non*. Did we find the toys? *Non*. Did we waste our time? *Oui*."

Uh, oh. Things were pretty bad when Camille played both sides of a conversation.

Grand-maman looked up from the counter where she was rolling out cookie dough. "François *non plus*," she said. "He did not find anything." She vigorously shook flour from a sifter onto her dough and clenched her rolling pin again, rolling it quickly over the dough.

Like Camille, *grand-maman* dropped her "Hs" and her "TH" blends sounded like double TTs making her last word come out like "anyTTing." The added emphasis on the second syllable gave her sentence a bit of bite that I suspected mirrored her mood. Which left me feeling even more guilty. If it hadn't been for me, the toys would all be safe and sound and hidden in the church basement, just waiting for the kids. Instead, all their gifts were at the mercy of would-be maple syrup thieves. And Christmas morning was only a little over a day away.

"Not to worry, *grand-maman*," a deep voice said from the doorway. "*Nous trouverons les cadeaux.*" Laurent. In a black sweater and jeans, leaning against the doorframe. The hair and voice of someone who just woke up even though he hadn't. As usual. And he seemed to be reassuring *grand-maman* that the toys would be found.

Camille dropped onto the bench at the table. "What are you doing here, big brother?"

His eyes flitted to me then over to her. "I'm here to help, of course."

François appeared behind Laurent. "I called him."

"*Naturellement*," Camille said with a shake of her head and a throaty sigh.

Grand-maman stopped mid-roll and shot Camille a stern look over her cookie dough.

I slid into a seat beside Camille. Setting aside whatever problem Camille had with her cousin, I for one was glad for the extra help. And I had no intention of letting us lose valuable time on a family squabble.

I scrounged in my pocket for a Christmas chocolate and passed it to Camille, her expression telling me she knew I was trying to pacify her with chocolate and my expression telling her to go along with it.

"It's good everyone's here," I said. "We need someone to run a check on the Beaulieu boys."

François ambled over to the counter where *grand-maman* worked, pilfered some cookie dough, and got a tap on the hand from *grand-maman*. He smiled and kissed the top of her head then turned his attention to me. "The Beaulieu boys?"

I nodded. "Gaétan and Pierre. You know them?"

"Every cop in the area knows them. They've been on the books since they were able to spit."

Laurent moved into the room, his eyes darkening, his muscles shifting to alert mode as PI stance took over. He pulled out the chair at the end of the table and sat, perched on the edge of the seat.

Grand-maman set aside her rolling pin and picked up a Christmas tree shaped cookie cutter covered in flour. "They are good boys the Beaulieus. Their *maman* died and they were upset." *Grand-maman* cut out a row of cookies and moved to the next. "They are not criminals, those two. They did little things, but no stealing. And they left for *université* more than two years ago."

Camille got up and went to get some coffee from the maker on the far counter, pouring the coffee into a large mug with Santa's face. "The boys are back, *grand-maman*. And they left the bar around the same time as your truck. Suspicious, no?"

Grand-maman waved a hand in the air the same way Camille did when dismissing an idea.

Laurent leaned in towards me, his voice low. "Is that the only lead?"

"So far," I told him.

He turned to François and said louder, "Then run them."

Grand-maman stopped cookie cutting, her floured hands hovering over her dough, her eyes darting a look of reproach Laurent's way. A look he skillfully avoided.

François, too, avoided eye contact with *grand-maman* as he pulled a phone from his pocket, punched a few keys, and headed towards the door that led to the dining room.

Camille leaned against a counter and sipped her coffee, watching him go.

And Laurent turned back to me, his attention focussed. "Tell me more about the Beaulieu boys."

I darted a glance at *grand-maman*. I so did not want to be the recipient of one of her glares. I'd wither away on the spot. The woman was kind and caring and wearing her wise-men apron again, which made being admonished by her all the more disconcerting. And judging by her furrowed brows as she vigorously wiped flour from her hands with a towel and marched over to the stove to tend the large pots she had simmering for dinner, the risk of a glare was high.

Laurent's eyes followed mine, and he shook his head and grabbed my hand, tugging me up and leading me out of the room.

He stopped walking when we reached the living room and let my hand drop. "Okay. Now tell me."

We were standing just inside the archway from the dining room, but there was no sign of François. Beyond Laurent, the sliding doors to the den were closed and I was guessing François was holed up on the other side. Aside from *grand-maman's* dogs, Princess and Simon, taking up their vigils by the fireplace, Laurent and I were alone while I filled him in on my conversation with pink-hair woman and purple nail-polish gal, adding in Hugo's pinpointing the time the Beaulieu boys had left the bar and our fruitless stops by the Beaulieu house and garage.

"It's not much," Laurent said when I was done, his gaze swaying from me to the ceiling now and then as he processed.

"I guess not," I agreed, trying to hide my disappointment. I'd seen Laurent find witnesses and long lost relatives given up for gone. As a PI, the man was practically a magician. Not that I expected him to pull more than half a dozen drums of maple syrup out of a hat or anything. But I was hoping he'd see our one lead as more than meets the eye. "But it's all we've got. It could be something, right?"

He nodded at me. Slowly. I knew that nod. That was his doubtful nod. Not good. In the morning I'd have to set my Plan B in motion—the plan that had been forming in my mind since the odds of finding the toys had fallen throughout the day—the plan to max out my credit cards buying up every toy I could get my hands on to replace the stolen ones. Admittedly, it wasn't a great plan—I only had two credit cards and neither had much left on them, but I'd replace as much as I could. I had to. I couldn't let all those kids on *grand-maman's* list be disappointed on Christmas morning.

"Your phone, Lora," I heard from behind me, pulling me from my thoughts.

I turned to see Camille holding my cell out to me. She must have fished it out of my purse back in the kitchen. "*C'est* Adam."

Adam. Right. With everything going on I'd forgotten he was taking the red eye back from California, and I was supposed to pick him up at the airport in the morning.

I took the phone. He wouldn't be too pleased to know I was still in *Trois-Rivières* and he'd have to take a taxi home on his own. Especially after the fuss I'd made about him going away at Christmastime.

"Hey," I said into the phone.

Camille raised an eyebrow at my sudden perky tone, and I shrugged. I had to go for perky if I was going to get through the call without a fight.

A minute later, I was raising my own eyebrow when Adam told me his flight was canceled because of fog in San Francisco. And with holiday travelers and all, he couldn't get another flight out until morning.

I smiled. This was the first bit of good luck I'd had. He wouldn't be home until late in the day, and I'd be home in time to pick him up after all. Either after we found the toys or after I replaced them. Stores were even open extra late with extended Christmas hours, maybe I wouldn't wait for morning. Maybe I'd go shopping after dinner.

I clicked off the call, still smiling about Adam's delay.

"You're happy Adam is not coming home?" Laurent said.

Naturally, with Laurent's nearly bionic ears it's no wonder he made out Adam's side of our phone conversation.

"Of course not," I said, stowing my phone in my jean's pocket. "And he *is* coming home, just a little later." I explained about the flight change and left it at that.

Camille sat in one of the rocking chairs that filled the living room and placed her arms on the side rests. "You didn't tell him you're still at *grand-maman's*, eh. Good move."

I flushed a little. I felt a tad guilty for not telling Adam about my own delay. But really, what was the point? I'd still be home before he was. "You think I should have?"

She grinned. "*Non, non.* This way you still win. It is not you who went out of the country at the holidays."

Sometimes it was scary the way Camille understood me. But sometimes it was also scary seeing myself through her eyes. Was I really that kind of girlfriend? The kind who wanted to come off looking better in an argument?

That's crazy. That's not what was happening here. My situation was completely different from Adam's. I wasn't working, I was trying to help little kids. Was it my fault a small mishap made that take longer? Well okay, technically maybe it was my fault, but it's not like I got the toys stolen on purpose.

I paced in a small circle, considering the idea of calling Adam back and telling him the truth.

Out of the corner of my eye, I saw Laurent watching me, his

look trailing up and back to me as I moved. Camille watched me, too, only her gaze didn't waver as she rocked in her chair, her expression a mix of curiosity and amusement.

Gee, so glad my life provided such entertainment for everyone.

Finally, I decided not to bother Adam and instead called our neighbor Joshua to make sure he could keep watching Ping and Pong until I got home. He agreed, insisting it was no trouble at all, and I got off the phone feeling relieved.

Even more so when *grand-maman's* voice announced from the kitchen that dinner was ready—the faster we ate, the faster I could get to my toy shopping.

I started for the dining room, and Camille jumped out of her chair, closed the distance to me in quick steps, and planted a kiss on my cheek, startling me into a full stop.

"What was that for?" I said.

She pointed up, and I followed her finger to a clump of mistletoe hanging from the wood-framed archway above my head.

Then I noticed Laurent mere steps behind me, rubbing the side of his torso. If I hadn't known better, I'd have thought Camille body-checked him on her way over to me. Siblings. Did they ever grow up? At times like this, I was almost glad I was an only child.

Grand-maman appeared in the dining room doorway that connected to the kitchen, her face impatient. "*Allez, les enfants*," she said. "*Vite*. I have much baking to do after *le souper*."

I checked my watch. Right. And I had a lot of toy shopping to do.

FRANÇOIS' PHONE PINGED halfway through our meal. He checked a text, shared it with Laurent, and the two men excused themselves. A possible lead they wanted to check out they said when they got their coats and Camille asked where they were going.

Grand-maman, too, had left the kitchen table and was readying for more baking. Only Camille and I lingered over our stews—mine vegetarian lentil and Camille's beef—sopping up the juicy remains with our buttered baguette.

I was soaking up my last bite when I heard *grand-maman* take in a sharp breath.

"*Qu'est-ce qu'il y a, grand-maman?*" Camille asked her, getting up and totting her dishes over to the dishwasher.

"*La garniture pour les biscuits,*" grand-maman said. "*J'en ai plus.*"

I had no idea what she said, but she didn't look happy about whatever it was.

"She has no more of the little red things that go on top of the cookies," Camille explained to me.

I got up and rinsed my dishes for the dishwasher, careful not to let the water spray too far. The counters were already filled with cookies—some frosted, some sprinkled, some layered, some cut into gingerbread men. Enough cookies to put the Keebler elves out of business. All sitting on racks, on plates, in half-filled tins. How many more cookies was *grand-maman* going to bake? Camille's family was big, but surely they couldn't put away all those cookies.

"You mean she's out of sprinkles?" I said.

Camille nodded. "The kids love them. *Grand-maman* is making cookies for the Christmas Eve party tomorrow at the church. Right after the family mass in the afternoon, there is always a gathering for everybody. I think some of the people come only for *grand-maman's* cookies. Every year she has to make more to keep up with the demand."

Ah. That explained why *grand-maman* had turned her kitchen into a cookie factory.

I stepped towards the wall hooks by the back door where we'd left out coats. "I'll go get some if I can borrow your car."

Camille reached for her purse, pulled out her keys, and tossed them to me.

I caught the keys, clenched them in my fist, and made my way out into the snowy night, grateful to be off on a useful errand. I may not be having any luck getting the toys back, but sprinkles I could get.

7

THERE WAS A supermarket close by in a strip mall on the edge of town. We passed it every time we drove the route to *grand-maman's* house. The mall was small with a bank at one end and the market at the other. In between, there was a pizza takeout place, a dollar store, a quickie haircut salon, and an empty storefront with an "*À Louer*" sign in the window. For rent. And by the looks of it, the space had been for quite some time.

I slid into a parking spot in front of the vacant store and went into the market. It was bright, mid-sized, and full of cheery Christmas music. It was also out of sprinkles. And according to the mime game punctuated by my broken French that I ended up in with the clerk, the store was not expected to get a new shipment before the holidays.

I left the store, went back to the Jetta, and used my phone to find the next nearest store. I was *not* going back to *grand-maman's* sans sprinkles. I couldn't let her down again.

Since there was little point in calling the store and checking stock—it being hard to mime over the phone and all—I kept the store location map up on my phone, set it on the seat beside me, and headed out. Seven minutes later, I pulled into another strip mall and left sans sprinkles. What was up with this town? Was a local band of Girl Guides churning out holiday cookies? Were all the store buyers really bad at projecting stock needs? It was Christmas for goodness sake. People needed their sprinkles.

I sat in the parking lot, called Camille, and told her my dilemma. She suggested I try one last place and gave me directions. I got there to find it was a convenience store. It was tucked into another edge of town and small, like the neighborhood bodega I grew up with back in Soho. And it had sprinkles. Lots of them. Red ones, green ones, along with silver balls and chocolate chimmies. I got them all and was humming a Christmas tune when I pulled away from the snowy curb, happy there'd be plenty of time left for toy shopping after I got the sprinkles back to *grand-maman*.

I was still humming and concentrating on reversing my tracks to get back to the more familiar end of town when I recognized the intersection leading to the Beaulieu garage and decided on a brief drive-by detour. Something still niggled at me about the place. I had no idea what. But something. And maybe seeing the place again would clue me in to what.

Beaulieu's was dark when I got there, the lot populated by a few cars near the garage bay and two more outside the office front. Loaners probably. Maybe the ones near the bay awaiting repairs.

I drove up to the building and slowed to cruise by both entrances. No sign of activity at either, and I was about to leave when I realized what bothered me. When I'd explored the place earlier with Camille, I'd noticed the building that housed the office front connected to the garage to the side, but it also extended much farther back than the garage. Even if I factored in some private spaces and washrooms beyond the front office, there was definitely some extra building booty going on.

Parking in the last slot in the loaner car row, I shoved my phone in my purse and got out to walk the pathway that led to the back of the building. With no driveway, walking was my only option, but in the full swing of evening it was turning cold. Camille's mom had been right; even my coat and vest combo wasn't enough to keep the chill out of my bones.

I rounded the building taking quick steps and hunkering into my coat collar, only to find another garage door in the back with its own driveway leading to the next street over. Fabulous. I was freezing for nothing, I could've come in that way by car.

Low light streamed out from inside the garage through a row of tiny windows, and I moved towards the light to look in, shifting into tiptoe mode, my eyes barely reaching the bottom of the window glass. Through the dirty pane, I could make out cars inside. Three of them. No. Make that two cars and one truck—*grand-maman's* ancient pickup with the peeling paint and cracked rear window. Bingo.

I backed away, rummaging in my purse for my cell phone, pausing when the light went out in the garage and the space around me darkened. The garage door hummed open and I jumped, my head whipping around, my eyes scanning for a hiding place as I sped over to a bank of snow and ducked down, cursing myself for wearing my purple coat and pom-pom hat. And cursing again when *grand-maman's* pickup chugged out of the garage and up towards the street.

I DASHED BACK to my car and sailed out of the parking lot, the Jetta's tires slipping in slush as I turned onto the road. The right blinker had been blinking on the pickup when I saw it leave, so I headed left to catch it around the block, hoping the truck hadn't gone too far, only to see it chug by in front of me when I reached the intersection.

I banged my hands on the steering wheel as the pickup left me behind at a red light. All I could do was watch it go and try to keep it in my sights. And try to keep my heart from jumping out of my chest.

Why oh why couldn't Québec allow right turns on a red light?

Finally, the light changed and I followed the pickup's path, trying not to lose it without getting too close. I propped up one knee to brace the steering wheel as I fumbled for my phone. Surely, the no-phone-while-driving rule didn't apply to emergencies. And this definitely qualified as an emergency.

Camille picked up on the first ring, and I shouted out the situation. I'd already made several more turns onto narrow roads leading farther out to rural areas with lots of trees and snow and few street signs. I had no idea where I was or where I was headed or who I was following. But I gave Camille my whereabouts as best I could, clicked off, and gripped the steering wheel with both hands. My neck stretched forward, my eyes straining to see in the dark and fluttering snow. Sprinkles schprinkles. I was going to bring *grand-maman* something better. Her stolen toys.

8

THE BACK OF the pickup was empty. No maple syrup barrels. No nothing. Which meant they'd already been unloaded. Somewhere. I only hoped the somewhere was the place I was headed.

I watched as *grand-maman's* truck turned into a lane with a mailbox at the entrance. I slowed and pulled to a stop a few yards from the lane, hiding behind giant pine trees dusted with snow. Idling, I waited a minute to see if the truck would come back out. When it didn't, I pressed redial on my phone and gave Camille an update. She dropped out in the middle of our call, my battery dead.

I had to believe she heard enough to figure out where I was and arrive soon for backup. Meanwhile, I edged the Jetta through a gap of trees I found a few yards away and cut the engine.

Five minutes later, the truck still hadn't come out. And Camille hadn't shown up. Not that I expected her to; I knew it would take longer for her to reach me out in the middle of nowhere. But sitting in wait was unsettling. With no properties lining the road, it was dark and devoid of traffic. And quiet except for a slight wind rustling the tree branches. Probably all big selling points when our thieves chose this as their lair, but spooky.

That's when it occurred to me this may not be a lair at all. For all I knew, the lane led to another road and *grand-maman's* pickup was making tracks on it as I sat freezing in Camille's Jetta. Through tree branches, I caught a partial view of the mailbox at the head of the lane and narrowed my eyes. Maybe the mailbox was a ruse. Maybe our thieves were really clever and put it there just to make it look like there was a house beyond the forest of trees. Too bad I hadn't gotten a better look at the mailbox. I could have checked the name, and if there was one, passed it along to Camille in case it helped her find me.

I could drive back over and have a look, maybe even cruise down the lane to see if there was a house down the way. But I didn't want to attract attention if there was, so I grabbed my purse, slung it across my shoulder to hug my body, grabbed the car keys, and got out to make my way over on foot.

And just as I suspected, there was no name on the mailbox.

My jaw tightened, and I turned a questioning eye to the laneway and pulled my hat down to cover my earlobes, adjusting the dangling bells from my pom-poms to minimize jingling. Then I started down the lane, keeping to the edge. The lane was long and winding with humongous, leafless trees to the sides making it feel almost like a tunnel. Snow had been cleared evenly in the center, either by a plow or a snow-blower, the banks waist high on either side. And it was dark, the moon hiding behind clouds, only the penlight I kept in my purse for emergencies or spontaneous sleuthing lighting my way.

A small clapboard house came into view when I rounded the last bend. Lights blazed in the front windows and smoke wafted from the chimney. *Grand-maman's* pickup nowhere in sight. And no other roads. The truck had to be around here somewhere.

I clicked off my penlight and shifted my weight to my toes, trying to minimize the scrunching of snow beneath my boots as I got closer to the house and crept up onto the veranda. I stood at the far end of the porch and stretched, peering through a slit the window curtains left bare. Inside, a giant TV screen played some Christmas movie I didn't recognize. And a woman sat on a couch, stroking a cat. And not just any woman. The woman from Beaulieu's garage, still wearing the same blue acrylic sweater.

What was she doing with *grand-maman's* pickup?

A list of possible explanations cycled through my brain, none of them coming up innocent.

I backed away from the window and left the veranda, creeping my way over to the detached garage—a converted outbuilding, also clapboard, with two sets of large wood doors latched together. Both sets locked, a scrap of red fabric poking out below the right door at the far end.

I smiled. I'd know that red fabric anywhere. The Caron Santa hat. And if Santa was inside it was a good bet the toys were, too. After all, Santa wouldn't stray far from his wares until he made his deliveries.

Behind me, light flooded on and beamed my way, sending me scurrying to the side of the building and crouching behind yet another snow pile. I tracked the light to a set of two floodlights attached high up on the main house, each fixture pointing towards a different zone of the property—the garage being one of them.

I froze, holding my breath, as the woman came out onto her porch, cat in her arms, and looked about. A moment later, she retreated back into the house and the lights flicked off.

My body shivered and my breathing resumed while I waited a bit longer to be sure she hadn't spotted me. Then I bolted farther back when the front door opened again, and the woman came out minus the cat and dressed in a parka and heavy duty boots, flash-light in hand.

Only it's hard to bolt through sticky, deep snow, so I found myself leaping into the shadows behind the outbuilding. Until one leap didn't land me in more snow—it sent me plunging down-wards for what seemed like an eternity, landing finally, feet first, backside second, in a dark pit.

I LOOKED UP and a clump of snow caught me in the face, more snow following after it adding to the snowy womb surrounding me, soft enough below to cushion my fall and thick enough around to provide surprising insulation from the cold.

A stream of light panned by overhead, and I sank back into my womb. It wouldn't be long before the woman spotted my boot holes in the snow. Nothing would give me away between the house and the garage—there were tracks everywhere there—but by the side of the building the snow had been pristine before I'd pulled my ten lords a leaping act.

My flight or fight response kicked in. Fat lot of good that it did. There was no way I was climbing out of a hole this deep and making a getaway. And aside from pelting the lady with snowballs, there was little I could do to defend myself. Especially if sweater lady didn't live alone and had rounded up a posse. I'd be outnum-bered. At least until my own posse showed up. Until then, my only hope was to burrow into the snow and pray sweater lady couldn't see me. Or that maybe she suffered from memory loss and wasn't sure if my tracks were fresh.

It grew dark above me as I weighed my options. And quiet. Maybe five minutes passed, and I thought maybe I'd gotten lucky and the woman had retreated to the house. Then I heard the slight but distinct sound of boots squishing snow, a faint echo reverberating with each step and drawing closer.

I started to scrape away at some loose snow beside me, my Isotoners getting wet and my fingers colder with every scrape. I packed the snow around me as best I could, like I was covering myself with damp sand at the beach. Not the best camouflage but better than nothing. The steps above grew louder, and I worked faster, putting my weight into the job, stifling a cry when I stubbed a finger on a chunk of ice. A chunk of ice that clicked and moved, then gave way and sent me plunging forward into another abyss.

9

I REACHED OUT to brace my fall and my arms knocked against what felt like knobby wood. My legs, too, hit something hard, my body bouncing a few times before coming to a complete stop as soft light came on, and I realized I wasn't in a hole at all. I was in a passageway. Crude and fashioned from cheap wood with minimal framing, a dirt floor, a string of small light fixtures several feet apart lining the ceiling. Behind me, a short snow-dusted ramp leading to my point of entry—what I could tell now was a small door. The tiny switch beside it the knobby bit I knocked into on my way in that must have brought on the lights.

I spied a latch on the door and scrambled up and over to close the door and slide the latch into place just in case sweater lady put two and two together and followed me in. I pulled my phone from my purse and tried powering it up on the off chance it had miraculously found new juice.

Unsurprisingly, it hadn't. Which left me with two choices: go back out the way I came in and face sweater lady or tap into my heretofore nonexistent spelunking skills and trek deeper into the passageway. Neither option appealed to me. The lady looked like she wouldn't take kindly to my "dropping in" and like she could make mighty use of that weighty flashlight she carried. On the other hand, the passageway probably *didn't* lead to Santa's work-shop and probably *did* provide house and home to many spiders, mice, and the like.

I shot one last look at the door, took in a musty deep breath, and headed into the passageway before I could change my mind. After only a few yards, a sharp, ninety-degree angle turn took me another several feet before I met another bend ahead, sans light bulbs. I stopped mid-step, hesitating. The bulbs hadn't given off much light but enough to make out creatures stirring in the night.

I peered at the dark in front of me. No way could I go in there without the lights. I really didn't want to run into creatures stir-ring in the night.

Then the faces of kids tucked up in their beds with visions of sugar plums danced in my head. The faces turning sad when they awoke to no toys under their trees.

"Ridiculous," I muttered to myself. "I can do this." I pulled my penlight from my pocket and tip-toed forward, panning my light back and forth, trying to ignore the fact that its thin beam didn't illuminate the cavern much.

After only half a dozen steps, I stopped again, my ears picking up a humming I hoped wasn't a swarm of bats coming my way, my hopes waning when I realized the sound was coming from above me. And along with my hopes, my bravery waned, too. I could do practically anything to help someone in need and definitely wanted the toys back for the kids, but I was beginning to realize I had a serious phobia of bats. Not to mention rats and mice and any creepy crawly larger than a dime. And I wasn't feeling too keen on dark, underground tunnels, either.

I made an effort to control my breathing and flashed my light towards the ceiling. No bats, just the humming.

Gingerly, I took a couple more steps, trusty penlight at the ready. The noise got louder still and morphed into voices when I found myself standing beneath another wood door. This one in the ceiling—the door small, square, and solid. Probably cheap plywood.

I tucked the penlight into the side of my hat and reached up towards the short rope that dangled from the door. That's when a large hand wrapped around mine and another hand wrapped around my mouth, muffling the squeal I automatically let loose. The same squeal that charged out of me when I spotted a huge spider in my shoe or felt a strand of hair on my shoulder that I was sure was some grotesque bug.

Strong arms surrounded me from the back and pulled my body snug into what would have been spooning position if our two bodies were horizontal.

I bucked backwards, trying to loosen my assailant's grasp, but the hold on me only got tighter. And there was a small chuckle near my ear. Warm, male, and familiar.

"*Calme-toi,* Lora. Hold still."

I stopped bucking and turned my head towards the voice to confirm what I already knew. Scruff grazed my cheek and intense eyes locked onto mine. A bright glint shooting through the eyes before they blinked closed and I was staring at the eyelids of Laurent Caron, mumbling to himself something that sounded suspiciously blasphemous.

The hand around my mouth released, moved upwards, and snatched the penlight from my hat.

"Hey," I said. "Take it easy or I'll tell your *grand-maman* that you took the Lord's name in vain."

He loosened his arm still clinging to my midsection and brought up his fingers to cover my mouth. "Shush."

Seriously? The man was shushing me when he was yacking away? That was so like him. Always inventing rules for me to follow. Important PI rules he felt obligated as my boss to teach me since I took the job at C&C. Only we weren't at work now and he was so not my boss. And if he was exempt from following the rules so was I.

I resisted the urge to bite his hand, glared at him, and peeled his fingers off my lips.

Before I could speak, he pointed upwards, and in the silence I heard the humming of voices above again and remembered I was in a cavern below the earth hunting down would-be maple syrup thieves turned toy Grinches. Which is when I wondered just how Laurent found me. Only I couldn't ask him because the "shush" rule was in effect.

One of the voices grew louder and a boot clomped onto the wood door mere inches from Laurent's head. Instinctively, I yanked him closer down to me, my hat scoring the move with a few notes of Jingle Bells.

Laurent's hand circled my head, squelching the bells, then he clicked off the penlight and clenched me to his body, his breath so close it melded with mine.

The voices were clear now and I could make out two—one male, one female. And even with my limited French I knew they were talking about some kind of trouble. Only judging by their tones they seemed to disagree on their plans to handle it.

I wasn't so clear on *our* plans to handle our trouble, either. With Laurent's whole shush thing going on, how were we supposed to figure out our next move? We couldn't just sit down here and let the Grinches above ruin Christmas for all those kids.

If this were some cartoon, we could flip open the trap door and send whoever was standing on it flying. Then we could go in guns blazing and round up the baddies.

Only this wasn't a cartoon. And we were in Canada. Nobody goes in guns blazing. Not even PIs carry guns unless they have special dispensation to do so. And even then, not often. Laurent did have a gun, but he rarely used it and I doubted he'd have brought it to *grand-maman's*. Which is probably why we were hunkered down here. Probably we were waiting for cousin François to show up with his big cop gun and maybe even some of his big cop friends. Cops here *were* allowed to carry guns. Which was good because the baddies didn't always pay attention to the no guns for citizens in Canada rule.

I felt a tap at my arm and heard the penlight click on. Its soft light pointed at the ground as Laurent gesticulated to the dark end of the passageway.

I looked into the darkness and back at Laurent. Did a big gulp and the words "ruh roh" mean anything to him? What was he thinking? I was fine and dandy right here thanks.

When I didn't move, he gestured again and shoved me forward a few steps and followed, keeping the light at his side aimed at the dirt floor ahead. I had no idea what his plan was, but this was definitely no time for ladies first. I tried to scramble behind him and got stuck in the "single-lane" only traffic. My tummy melded onto his hip and I wiggled to get loose, my hat starting up another bar of Jingle Bells.

Laurent yanked off my hat and shoved it in his pocket, a gush of warm air hitting my head as he let out another blasphemous remark. The penlight glow dimmed, and his arms braced mine while he shimmied me behind him and started walking again, one hand pulling mine, the other holding the light.

We moved through another bend and got to another trap door in the ceiling, this one quiet on the other side.

Laurent passed me the penlight, holding his hand over mine until the light was trained on the trap door. Then he let go and went to work opening the door. Wafts of dust flew down when the door flipped up, and I simultaneously stifled a cough and a sneeze, dropping the light in the process. When I picked it up and pointed it back up to the door, Laurent had hoisted himself up enough that he could see into the space above.

Silently, he edged himself back down and reached for me, his hands grasping my waist so fast I was up and through the trap door opening before I could so much as get another urge to sneeze.

10

"**N**OW WHAT?" **I** mouthed to Laurent.

We were standing in a small space with boxes piled around the perimeter. A storage locker by the looks of it. Darkened but organized, the naked light bulb dangling from the low ceiling switched off but swaying.

Laurent made the shush sign over his lips, stilled the light, resealed the trap door, and moved towards a wall of boxes. Quietly, he lifted the top boxes and placed them on the floor to the side. Then he leaned over the remaining boxes and put his ear to the wall.

While he was busy with that I kept the penlight low, made my way over to the narrow door, and got in listening mode, too. I could hear the same Grinch voices, faint but still raised and clipped.

I turned back to Laurent and saw he had retreated from the wall and was texting on his cell phone. His fingers stopped moving, his eyes still trained on the phone, and I wondered who was on the other end and just how long their interchange would take. Now that I was out of the creepy cavern, I itched to find the toys. Plus, without my hat, I was cold. The locker was clearly poorly insulated and possibly unheated. And it didn't smell all that good, either.

I went over to Laurent and reached into his pocket for my hat. Without taking his gaze off his phone, he shook his head and clamped his pocket so the hat wouldn't budge. I tugged some more but lost my grip and toppled backwards onto a box, landing on it in sit position then feeling it give way. I sank into it, the sides ripping under my weight, and cigarettes spilled out of the box and onto the floor around me.

Mere seconds later, the storeroom door burst open and sweater lady and some younger guy came in. The bickering Grinches, no doubt.

Laurent stepped in front of me, his phone gone from sight, his shoulders squared, his legs planted.

I craned my head to peek through the gap between Laurent's lower legs. Sweater lady wore the same ensemble as earlier, complete with flashlight, along with a new look of shock. The guy beside her, small and wiry with stick legs in corduroy pants, wore a parka with the hood up and a nasty scar to the side of his mouth giving him a permanent sneer.

Wiry guy surveyed the cigarettes and swore. Sweater lady fidgeted with her flashlight and whispered something towards him that got a nod from wiry guy who pulled a knife from his pocket and triggered the blade.

Sweater lady took one last look at us and left. Wiry guy stepped into the room, his back to the open door and gestured with his knife for us to go out after her.

I struggled to get out of the broken box. Laurent extended his hand to help me, and wiry guy shouted something at him in French and waved his knife around. Laurent said something back, sounding calm, old cop voice in place, and pulled his hands away from me and up, presumably to show they were empty.

Wiry guy gestured at the doorway again. "Mon amie va appeller la police dans deux minutes si vous êtes encore ici."

I understood two things from that sentence: one, that if we didn't leave immediately, sweater lady was going to call the police; and two, that wiry guy was a big bluffer. No way were they calling the police on us when they were the ones housing *grand-maman's* stolen pickup and scads of Santa toys. Not to mention the cigarettes. I was willing to bet more of these boxes were filled with cigarettes, and I doubted they were all for personal use. Nobody had a smoking addiction that bad. And who knew what else there may be stored here. After all, these people were willing to steal maple syrup—their province's very own oil—and take precious income away from their fellow workers. Talk about sad saps.

And maybe none-too-bright sad saps, either, if they took us as trespassers or would-be thieves who would be so intimidated by a wiry guy waving a knife around and threatening us with the police that we'd leave and never come back. If indeed that's what they planned for us.

But I followed Laurent's lead and pretended to believe wiry guy. I knew Laurent could have taken this guy out in two seconds if he'd wanted to. If he hadn't, he had good reasons. Probably not knowing how many other wiry guys with weapons may show up was one of them. Laurent never took action until he fully scoped out a situation. He took great pains to avoid collateral damage. Plus, he liked to win. And it was way easier to win when he knew the odds he was playing against.

I maneuvered myself up and went out the door, Laurent behind me, and behind him wiry guy. We passed into an area with two other doors, one adjoining the storeroom and one centered on the opposite wall. Glancing into the nearest room, I saw our maple syrup tubs. But wiry guy was prompting us to enter the centered door, which turned out to be the garage with the large double doors and *grand-maman's* pickup truck.

I pretended to trip before I got through the doorway. I was *not* leaving without Santa and his toys.

Laurent knocked into me, and I caught his eye and glanced towards the maple syrup barrels.

His eyes barely moved, but I knew he'd seen the tubs, so I was surprised when he pushed me onward. Hard. His body continuing to ram mine with enough force to propel me nearly halfway across the garage.

When I turned back to object, I saw why. A snarly Doberman raced out of the room that had the maple syrup barrels and headed straight for me.

11

THE DOG HAD me easily equalled in weight. And height, as he stood on hind legs, lunged at my shoulders, and knocked me down. His nose burrowed into my belly and poked around giving me a good tenderizing.

It all happened so fast, nobody had moved until I was on the floor, and I saw Laurent step forward and wiry guy try to restrain him.

Up close, the dog's face lost its snarl and took on a look of focus and determination. His snout drilled harder into my side, his collar tags jangling, his mouth starting to drool from one side. A deep growl reached my ears, and I looked down at the dog, his tag dangling, the name "Balzac" marked in block letters. He lifted his head, his ears perked up, and his eyes connected with mine as he let out a whine and curled up in my lap, shaking slightly.

The growl grew louder, and I looked around to place it since it clearly wasn't coming from Balzac. I didn't see another dog, but I did see Laurent coming at us at full force. He swept both Balzac and me to the wall of the garage just as the double doors crashed open and Camille's Jetta drove in, stopping halfway through the doors and just short of *grand-maman's* pickup. Camille jumped out of her car and scanned the garage, nabbing wiry guy by his parka hood when he tried to dash out.

Wiry guys hands flew to his head and he cried out, making me think Camille had nabbed some hair along with the hood.

François squeezed through the gap between the door and the Jetta. He looked first towards Laurent, Balzac, and I huddled on the floor then over at Camille and wiry guy.

"Someone going to explain?" François said.

Wiry guy started yelling and pointing at Laurent and me.

François turned his gaze on us and back to wiry guy. "Okay. *Et pourrais-tu m'expliquer pourquoi ce camion est ici?*"

I rolled my eyes. Wiry guy must still be playing his sad sap role and trying to blame us for this mess. But François was asking him about *grand-maman's* truck. I couldn't wait to hear how he explained that. Not to mention the maple syrup tubs filled with Santa and the toys.

I moved to get up and Balzac pawed my coat, whined again, and sat at my feet when I was fully standing. Laurent stood, too, and told François about sweater lady and the stash of cigarettes, walking over to him as he spoke and filling him in on more details in lower tones.

At the mention of sweater lady, Camille let out a whistle and cocked her chin in the direction of the Jetta where, sure enough, sweater lady sat in the back seat, her expression grim, her hair mussed, and no doubt her hands and feet tied.

More cops came in behind François, these ones in uniform. After an interchange with François, one cuffed wiry guy, and another pulled sweater lady from Camille's car, disposed of Camille's improv shackles, and cuffed the lady. The other cops headed into the back rooms.

Balzac nuzzled at my coat some more, and it finally dawned on me what he was after—not me, but the contents of my pockets still stocked with treats I kept for my own dog. I fished one out and tossed it to Balzac, who batted his tail back and forth so hard in response that he nearly knocked me over again. I patted his head, shivered, and settled deeper into my coat, the cold of the doorless garage getting to me.

"Don't even think about it," Camille said as she came over, her eyes taking full inventory of my condition before resting on Balzac. "You do not need another mutt."

"Oh Balzac's not a mutt. He's a purebred." I looked down at him again. "At least I think so."

When I looked up again, Laurent had joined us. "Okay. We go, eh." His eyes met mine and he paused, pulling my hat from his pocket and placing it on my head. "Next case, we get you a hat without bells."

"*Laisse-la*, Laurent," Camille said, reaching up to jingle my bells. "She wasn't on a case. She can wear whatever she wants." She crooked her arm through mine. "But we do have to go. *Grand-maman* is waiting for those sprinkles."

12

"*I* LOOK RIDICULOUS." I stood back and studied myself in the large antique standing mirror in *grand-maman's* guest room. So much for wearing what I want.

This is what I got for travelling light. Good thing I always packed extra underwear or I'd have been going commando for our extended stay instead of just borrowing a dress.

Camille started walking for the door. "*Mais voyons*, Lora. You can't go to church in jeans. *Grand-maman* would have a fit. Let's go already."

Easy for her to say. She was wearing a long, red wool sweater dress she kept at her grandmother's for emergencies. Emergencies having to do with church going it seemed.

I was dressed in a long-sleeved polyester dress in a dark flower print with a doily collar one of her cousin's kept at the house. Presumably for Amish gatherings circa 1910.

"It wouldn't be so bad if you opened the collar." Camille stepped back over to me and worked the buttons at my neck. "*Tu vois. C'est pas si mal.*"

I checked the mirror to see if she was right and the dress wasn't as bad as it was a minute ago. Now I had a frilly "V" that showed the thin silver-chained necklace *grand-maman* had given me when we'd brought the toys back the night before. The chain had a tiny cross hanging from it, the first one I'd ever had. I'd give Camille improvement on the necklace front. It was certainly way better than a doily.

If Camille hadn't been at least half a foot taller than me, I would have rock paper scissored her for the red dress, but since the dress was long most of it would be trailing on the floor if I wore it. Like Morticia Adam's dress, only red. I couldn't imagine that would go over well in church, either.

A small tap came at the door and François cleared his throat. "*Vite*, Camille. *Grand-maman* wants you to help load the cookies."

Camille went to open the door and François tipped forward slightly, taking a stumbling step into the room. She glared at him. "You still have zero respect for privacy, eh François? Why don't *you* go help *grand-maman* before I teach you another lesson."

François grimaced, and I pretended to fuss some more with my dress while I listened. That crack about privacy was the first clue I had about the grudge Camille seemed to harbor towards François.

"*Grand-maman* doesn't want my help," François said. "She asked for you."

"*Quelle surprise*," Camille said. "*Probablement* she thinks you'll drop the cookie tins." She got her purse from the bed and headed out to the hall.

I grabbed my own purse and caught up with them. "Wait. I'll go with you. I can help, too." And if I stuck real close, maybe, just maybe, I'd finally learn more about their old feud.

. . .

WHEN WE GOT DOWNSTAIRS, I hadn't scored any more clues in Françoisgate, and *grand-maman* insisted I relax in the living room instead of helping cart cookies out to the car. Just like she insisted I stay for the Christmas Eve afternoon church services so I could meet some of the kids who would be the happy recipients of our recovered toys. *Grand-maman* was in high spirits with the gifts back and the Beaulieu brothers in the clear, both proving her faith in the power of good as far as she was concerned. And since I could relate to that sentiment, I felt we shared a bond.

As much as I was loving my first taste of a French Christmas, though, I had mixed feelings about her inviting me to stay for church. Like the rest of the women in Camille's clan, *grand-maman* knew I had no family left and was making the effort to include me in theirs. Which was nice. But hanging around for the afternoon meant I couldn't pick Adam up at the airport when his flight from California got in, and he'd definitely have to taxi it home. Plus, with the whole family staying on later for Christmas Eve dinner, I'd have to borrow someone's car to get home, and I'd be cutting it close even for dinner with Adam.

"*Chocolat* for your thoughts?"

I smiled and looked up from the couch at Laurent who stood in front of me, a slight bend at his waist, candy dish extended towards me. I gave him brownie points for not making fun of my dress and picked a chocolate mint wafer out of the dish. "Sure. That's way better than a penny. You Carons really know how to sweeten the deal."

He snatched a wafer for himself, set the dish back on the side table, and sat beside me. "It's the least we can do for your help in getting the toys and *grand-maman's* truck back."

I looked down at my lap. "I'm not sure falling in a hole qualifies as helping. Camille did most of the work by rounding up the bad guys."

"You didn't fall in a hole. That was a stairwell leading to an old root cellar. If it hadn't been buried in snow, you'd have seen the stairs. And, it is you, Lora, who *found* the bad guys."

True maybe, but mostly that was just good timing. I may have had my suspicions about Beaulieu's garage, but I didn't suspect sweater lady. Or her accomplice, wiry guy, who it turns out was an ex-employee of Beaulieu's who quit to pursue his more lucrative career in the black market, leaving Monsieur Beaulieu high and dry at the holidays. And *grand-maman* sans pickup and toy donations.

"Do you think that wiry guy really took *grand-maman's* truck thinking it was loaded with maple syrup?" I asked Laurent.

"You mean Claude Brodeur? *Oui*, it seems so. He saw the truck when he was on his way to the bar to meet his friends, the Beaulieu brothers. He's the one who left that wreck of a car behind. Also stolen. With his expertise in cars, he stole them now and then for parts. But coming across the maple syrup was a much better deal."

I could understand that. Kind of like the chocolate/penny thing. Only I couldn't imagine that clunker he'd been driving having any parts worth salvaging. "What about the gas? *Grand-maman's* truck was empty when we left it."

"Probably he siphoned some out of the stolen car and used that."

Hmm. "And there's really a black market for maple syrup?"

Laurent nodded. "There's a black market for just about everything. Including the cigarettes and other goodies we found. Our Monsieur Brodeur was small time, but he was getting in deep. That's why he partnered up with the office lady from Beaulieu's. He needed more storage. Her husband left her with two mortgages and no savings. She needed extra cash and Brodeur rented space from her. She had no idea what he was really up to until she came across the pickup filled with toys and he had to explain."

Poor sweater lady. Duped by two men. One who stole her time and one who got her time.

François ambled into the living room munching on a cookie. No wonder *grand-maman* didn't ask for his help loading the cookies into the car. She wasn't afraid he'd drop them, she was afraid he'd eat them.

"It's almost time to go," he said.

Laurent stood and offered me a hand up. "I'm surprised you're still here, François. I thought for sure Camille would have taken you out again by now."

François smiled. "Not this time. We're not kids anymore, and she is not the only one who knows how to take a man out. She won't try anything now."

"Camille took François out when you were kids?" I asked.

"She didn't tell you?" Laurent said. "When she was ten and François was fifteen. She was already a black belt. François stole her diary and read it to his friends." Laurent laughed. "He did not read anything else for a long while. But he did learn how to keep a secret."

So that's what happened. I couldn't help but smile. That's my girl. Only François was wrong about her, she would still take him out today if she had good reason whether he was trained or not. His training would only make her undoubted victory all the sweeter.

"Obviously I can keep a secret better than you, cousin." François strolled over and grabbed a mint from the dish. "But I could make an exception for Lora here." He pointed at me with his chocolate but was looking at Laurent. "Like maybe she'd want to know why the house of *grand-maman* looks like a *jardin de mistletoe* this year."

I looked from one to the other, wondering what this new secret was about, this time wishing I hadn't been an only child. I may have missed out on a lot of fights, but I also missed out on a lot of sharing.

And would apparently still be missing out on this particular sharing if the fire Laurent's eyes were directing at François had anything to do with it.

"*Regarde,* Lora. *Un autre cadeau pour toi.* Another early Christmas present for you."

I turned at hearing Camille's voice, leaving all hopes of learning the mistletoe secret behind.

Camille waved her arm in a ta-da motion to her side, and in walked Adam. His cheeks still flushed from outside, his shirt and jeans as ruffled as his short hair, and a small wrapped box in his hands.

My heart sped up looking at the box. It was jewelry sized, the bow nearly dwarfing the box.

I went towards Adam, my hand giving calming pats to my chest. "How did you get here?"

"Camille called me," he said, wrapping me in a hug when I reached him. "She invited me to some church thing and said you'd need a ride home afterwards." He let me go and held out the box. "Here. I got this for you in San Francisco."

I could feel all eyes in the room on me as I took the box. Even *grand-maman* had come in and Princess and Simon had their heads perked up and watching.

Slowly I lifted the lid, taking small breaths. I wasn't sure what I'd find in the box or if I'd be ready for whatever it was. There was tissue paper inside and under the paper, a silver bracelet with three tiny charms: an Empire State building, a Statue of Liberty, and a subway token.

"You like it?" Adam asked. "I thought it would remind you of home."

A long breath escaped me and my heart calmed. I could have sworn I heard a breath come out of Camille, too, who'd come up to stand beside me and helped me fasten the bracelet around my wrist.

"It's lovely," I told Adam. "I love it." And I did, only looking around *grand-maman's* warm house at all the faces around me, the bracelet didn't feel so much like a reminder of home anymore.

I felt Adam's arms come around me and he gave me a long kiss. "Mistletoe," he said, pointing up and smiling when he pulled away. "You were standing right under it."

⚜

SNEAK PEEK AT MORE LORA!

Curious how Lora met the Carons?

Find out in the Lora Weaver series prequel, *The Demi-Tasse Début*.

The Demi-Tasse Début

CHAPTER ONE

A PICK-UP LINE in any other language is still a pick-up line.

Even if I didn't understand a word of it.

I looked up at the man speaking to me in French. He was tall with shoulders broad enough to suggest he worked out but not so broad to suggest he mixed steroids into his orange juice at breakfast. He was dressed in a T-shirt and jeans and wore scuffed sandals that looked like they'd just come from a day at the beach.

With a demure shake of my head, I offered him a low *non merci,* but he remained standing to the side of the teensy table where I sat in the teensy café that had beckoned me in with its vintage mismatched chairs and vibrant mismatched coffee cups. And maybe most importantly of all, its whirring air-conditioning. After the morning I'd had, I was in desperate need of a reprieve from the sauna outdoors trying to pass itself off as just another summer's day.

If I'd known summers in Montréal could be just as smoldering as back in New York, I never would have moved here. Okay, maybe that's not true. I agreed faster than it took me to blink when my boyfriend, Adam, had asked me to accompany him to his hometown. And when it wasn't playing mix'n'match with blistering heat and sweltering humidity, I loved the city. From its cobblestone walkways to its vast parklands to its array of one-way-streets. I loved the museums and the endless summer street festivals and the French air of *je ne sais quoi* that made strolling in the park seem far more essential than running the rat race.

I heard the rustle of chair feet on tile floor and pick-up-line man sat down across from me, pulled out a journal, and began jotting notes in the pages. Not looking at me even once.

The tingly warmth on my skin, faded thanks to the air-conditioning, started to flame again. Maybe I had it wrong. Maybe the guy just wanted a place to sit. Perfect strangers shared tables all the time in popular restaurants during busy times. And one perusal of the place told me it was definitely busy time. Nary an empty seat in sight. Maybe I had misunderstood the pick-up line after all. Since arriving in Montréal, I'd brushed away over a dozen years of dust from my high-school French and trotted it out gleefully only to realize my teacher had been generous with my C grade for the class. Maybe what the guy had asked was more like "Is this seat taken?" and the shake of my head gave him the go-ahead to join me.

I rearranged my *mochaccino glacé* and croissant in front of me, fidgeting to hide my embarrassment. Jumping to conclusions was not a sport I played often. Or well, apparently.

I went back to the novel I'd brought with me to read on the métro. The carnation, bought earlier from a street vendor for luck and tucked into the book's pages, still marked the same place it had then, my mind too tense to read on the way downtown and too dejected after I'd left my appointment. A job interview. The latest in a string of interviews that went exactly the same. My education, impeccable. My nearly ten years experience as a social worker in New York, impressive. My lack of French skills, impassable. As in a deal-breaker. A roadblock, as it were, to my getting any position in a city that requires bilingualism for jobs in my field. Or possibly, stellar unilingual skills, so long as that uni language is French.

"It's not personal," one interviewer had said. "It's just the law here for organizations like us. We can't hire candidates without at least some good French." A sympathetic smile capped her words.

I'd smiled back, clutching the sheet of references I'd brought that would once again go unused, wanting to ask if she might be so kind as to list any organizations that may hire candidates like me. But I knew better than to bother. Having already sat through identical conversations at other interviews, I feared the answer would be a confused look and a head shake. If there were any social work jobs in Montréal that accepted English-only workers like me I was sure the jobs would be few and far between, in high demand, and likely once secured, kept until retirement.

I perched my book at the edge of the café table, beside my croissant plate, and made myself read a paragraph. Either I could sit here and brood about my unemployment or I could escape into the British countryside and manor house life of the nineteenth century, and I was choosing escape.

Every few words my eyes drifted upwards, to my table mate's notebook, the zip of his pen crossing the small pages in swift streaks, his movement causing our table to rock onto its one short leg and back again. The man's head bent forward and his hair, wound at the crown like dark rotini, dipped so close to me I caught a hint of musky scent from his shampoo.

I peered at his scrawl, a skeletal printing tough to make out upside down. Not English I thought. But same alphabet. Likely French, or Italian maybe, definitely some kind of accents over letters.

At the end of a page, he paused and checked a text on his phone then flipped the book closed, drank down his espresso in one shot like it was booze, and looked straight at me.

I smiled, hoping he hadn't noticed my brief perusal of his notes. My chair jostled, once and then again, and I let my eyes travel from the man to the ground where a white rubber wheel ensnared my chair leg. The wheel belonged to a stroller. The stroller to a young mom with a toddler snoozing, chin to chest in the seat, and another child, a girl maybe five years old, sweaty, one elbow held aloft smeared with dirt and fresh blood. The girl dragged a scooter and wore a bright pink helmet tilted sideways on her head, straps dangling open at her neck. Tendrils escaped the mom's tangerine braid of hair, her skin glistened, and her eyes had the look of someone in desperate need of caffeine. And a place to rest her weary feet.

I stood to untangle the wheel from my chair and whisked my book back into my bag. "Here," I said. "Take my seat. I'm just finishing up."

The mom glanced at my nearly-full *mochaccino glacé* and my uneaten croissant.

"No really," I said. "I, um, was going to move to the patio to get some sun." Okay, this was a lie, but lies didn't count when they were white ones for good causes.

The girl limped to my chair and sat, taking me at my word.

While she hopped up, I held the wood back of the chair firmly, noticing that my pick-up-line friend had vacated his side of the table and was nowhere to be seen. Quickly I gathered up his leftover espresso cup and my own things and smiled at the mom who gratefully sank into the man's vacant chair and thanked me, her accent French but her words perfect English.

I thought of offering to watch the toddler while the mom took the girl to the bathroom to wash off her bloody elbow but knew that babysitting may not be a welcome suggestion from a stranger, so I offered to get her some wet napkins instead. She declined, thanking me again, and withdrew a package of moist wipes from the diaper bag draped over the stroller handlebars. She passed the wipes to her daughter who cleaned up her own boo-boo, topping it with the animal print bandage her mother doled out automatically in follow-up. In the preparedness department, Boy Scouts had nothing on mothers. Mothers with diaper bags were like turtles with shells. Wherever they went, they carried all the comforts of home. Or at least the important ones.

The mom dropped the daughter's used wipe into a tiny bag draped from the side of the stroller near a cup holder. She pulled a coloring book and set of crayons from the mess of toys and books brightly covered in flowers, trucks, and kittens crammed into a basket below the snoozing child, and she passed the crayons to the little girl who waved me off with a shy smile.

To make good on my lie, I went out to the patio, more courtyard than terrace, surprised to find it, too, quite crowded. Flagstones on the ground, the area was longer than it was wide, the width as narrow as the café interior, the length longer, extending outward buffered by a brick wall at the end, the rest lined by a short iron fence, intertwining vines covering the iron in lush green. On the outer side of the fence hung flower boxes with bright pink and white flowers. Courtyard side, marble-topped bistro tables clustered with narrow chairs made the most of every square inch, most already taken, but I managed to snag a table close to the café door, hoping to catch wafts of air-conditioning streaming out as people came and went.

Two bites into my croissant, a shadow darkened my table. Another man, glare of sun behind him catching me in the eye when I looked up.

I waited a beat for him to speak, not wanting to jump to conclusions again, hoping this newcomer and I spoke the same language. This time, whatever the guy wanted had to be more than a seat because there were empty tables to be had.

To lessen the glare in my eyes and see the guy better, I reached down to where I'd left my purse on the ground beside me, fishing for the sunglasses I'd hooked onto the straps. The shadow above me loomed closer, swooped down, and in a flash my bag was gone. Nothing left but my department store shades dangling from my fingertips.

***

End of Sample
Full book is Available Now!

ACKNOWLEDGMENTS

I am infinitely grateful for the support of my betas, family, and friends. Also to Maud L. for adding her special touch to the French bits.

But a special thanks goes to all my readers, especially those who have taken the time to write me or share their love of the Lora Weaver books with their friends. *Merci* all for helping me bring the Lora Weaver world to life:)

ABOUT THE AUTHOR

Katy Leen is the author of the Lora Weaver mystery novels. She credits her mom for sparking her lifelong love of stories through her own avid love of books. When she's not writing, Katy can be found listening to bookish podcasts, delving into all things wellness, reading, or hanging out with her hubby and family—always with a pup at her side and a cup of cocoa nearby.

Join Katy's *Nouvelles* newsletter where she shares more meanderings and insider info about the books:)

Pop by katyleen.com to check out the Q&A and her blog or Follow Katy at:

ALSO BY KATY LEEN

Series in Order

The First Faux Pas

The Nearly Nixed Noël (holiday novella)

The Pas de Deux

The Lost Love Liaison (Valentine novella)

The Ménage à Trois

The Easter Egg Ennui (Easter novella)

The Petit-Four Score

More Books

The Demi-Tasse Début (prequel novella)

The Bonne Année Brouhaha (holiday novella)

Bundle Books

The Lora Weaver Bundle

The Lora Weaver Holiday Boxed Set

The Lora Weaver series is still growing! Pop over to Katy's website for news about the latest books.

The series is available in print, ebook, and audiobook.

I hope you join me for more of Lora's adventures:)

Happy reading!

www.ingramcontent.com/pod-product-compliance
Lightning Source LLC
Chambersburg PA
CBHW071342130626
46556CB00005B/1993